Heinrich Zschokke

The Broken Cup

Outlook

Heinrich Zschokke

The Broken Cup

1. Auflage | ISBN: 978-3-73261-804-0

Erscheinungsort: Paderborn, Deutschland

Erscheinungsjahr: 2018

Outlook Verlag GmbH, Paderborn.

Heinrich Zschokke

The Broken Cup

Outlook

THE BROKEN CUP

By Johann Heinrich Daniel Zschokke

Translated by P. G.

⎯⎯⎯⎯⎯⎯⎯⎯⎯⎯⎯⎯⎯

Author's Note.—There is extant under this name a short piece by the author of "Little Kate of Heilbronn." That and the tale which here follows originated in an incident which took place at Bern in the year 1802. Henry von Kleist and Ludwig Wieland, the son of the poet, were both friends of the writer, in whose chamber hung an engraving called *La Cruche Cassée*, the persons and contents of which resembled the scene set forth below, under the head of The Tribunal. The drawing, which was full of expression, gave great delight to those who saw it, and led to many conjectures as to its meaning. The three friends agreed, in sport, that they would each one day commit to writing his peculiar interpretation of its design. Wieland promised a satire; Von Kleist threw off a comedy; and the author of the following tale what is here given.

⎯⎯⎯⎯⎯⎯⎯⎯⎯⎯⎯⎯⎯

Contents

MARIETTA.

NAPOULE, it is true, is only a very little place on the bay of Cannes; yet it is pretty well known through all Provence. It lies in the shade of lofty evergreen palms, and darker orange trees; but that alone would not make it renowned. Still they say that there are grown the most luscious grapes, the sweetest roses, and the handsomest girls. I don't know but it is so; in the mean time I believe it most readily. Pity that Napoule is so small, and can not produce more luscious grapes, fragrant roses, and handsome maidens; especially, as we might then have some of them transplanted to our own country.

As, ever since the foundation of Napoule, all the Napoulese women have been beauties, so the little Marietta was a wonder of wonders, as the chronicles of the place declare. She was called the *little* Marietta; yet she was not smaller than a girl of seventeen or thereabout ought to be, seeing that her forehead just reached up to the lips of a grown man.

The chronicles aforesaid had very good ground for speaking of Marietta. I, had I stood in the shoes of the chronicler, would have done the same. For Marietta, who until lately had lived with her mother Manon at Avignon, when she came back to her birthplace, quite upset the whole village. Verily, not the houses, but the people and their heads; and not the heads of all the people, but of those particularly whose heads and hearts are always in danger when in the neighborhood of two bright eyes. I know very well that such a position is no joke.

Mother Manon would have done much better if she had remained at Avignon. But she had been left a small inheritance, by which she received at Napoule an estate consisting of some vine-hills, and a house that lay in the shadow of a rock, between certain olive trees and African acacias. This is a kind of thing which no unprovided widow ever rejects; and, accordingly, in her own estimation, she was as rich and happy as though she were the Countess of Provence or something like it.

So much the worse was it for the good people of Napoule. They never suspected their misfortune, not having read in Homer how a single pretty woman had filled all Greece and Lesser Asia with discord and war.

HOW THE MISFORTUNE CAME ABOUT.

Marietta had scarcely been fourteen days in the house, between the olive trees and the African acacias, before every young man of Napoule knew that she lived there, and that there lived not, in all Provence, a more charming girl than the one in that house.

Went she through the village, sweeping lightly along like a dressed-up angel, her frock, with its pale-green bodice, and orange leaves and rosebuds upon the bosom of it, fluttering in the breeze, and flowers and ribbons waving about the straw bonnet, which shaded her beautiful features—yes, then the grave old men spake out, and the young ones were struck dumb. And everywhere, to the right and left, little windows and doors were opened with a "Good morning," or a "Good evening, Marietta," as it might be, while she nodded to the right and left with a pleasant smile.

If Marietta walked into church, all hearts (that is, of the young people) forgot Heaven; all eyes turned from the saints, and the worshiping finger wandered idly among the pearls of the rosary. This must certainly have provoked much sorrow, at least, among the more devout.

The maidens of Napoule particularly became very pious about this time, for they, most of all, took the matter to heart. And they were not to be blamed for it; for since the advent of Marietta more than one prospective groom had become cold, and more than one worshipper of some beloved one quite inconstant. There were bickerings and reproaches on all sides, many tears, pertinent lectures, and even rejections. The talk was no longer of marriages, but of separations. They began to return their pledges of troth, rings, ribbons, etc. The old persons took part with their children; criminations and strife spread from house to house; it was most deplorable.

Marietta is the cause of all, said the pious maidens first; then the mothers said it; next the fathers took it up; and finally all—even the young men. But Marietta, shielded by her modesty and innocence, like the petals of the rosebud in its dark-green calix, did not suspect the mischief of which she was the occasion, and continued courteous to everybody. This touched the young men, who said, "Why condemn the pure and harmless child—she is not guilty!" Then the fathers said the same thing; then the mothers took it up, and finally all—even the pious maidens. For, let who would talk with Marietta, she was sure to gain their esteem. So before half a year had passed, everybody had spoken to her, and everybody loved her. But she did not suspect that she was the object of such general regard, as she had not before suspected that she was the object of dislike. Does the violet, hidden in the downtrodden grass, think how sweet it is?

Now every one wished to make amends for the injustice they had done Marietta. Sympathy deepened the tenderness of their attachment. Marietta found herself greeted everywhere in a more friendly way than ever; she was more cordially welcomed; more heartily invited to the rural sports and dances.

ABOUT THE WICKED COLIN.

All men, however, are not endowed with tender sympathy; some have hearts hardened like Pharaoh's. This arises, no doubt, from that natural depravity which has come upon men in consequence of the fall of Adam, or because, at their baptism, the devil is not brought sufficiently under subjection.

A remarkable example of this hardness of heart was given by one Colin, the richest farmer and proprietor in Napoule, whose vineyards and olive gardens, whose lemon and orange trees could hardly be counted in a day. One thing particularly demonstrates the perverseness of his disposition; he was twenty-seven years old, and had never yet asked for what purpose girls had been created!

True, all the people, especially damsels of a certain age, willingly forgave him this sin, and looked upon him as one of the best young men under the sun. His fine figure, his fresh, unembarrassed manner, his look, his laugh, enabled him to gain the favorable opinion of the aforesaid people, who would have forgiven him, had there been occasion, any one of the deadly sins. But the decision of such judges is not always to be trusted. While both old and young at Napoule had become reconciled to the innocent Marietta, and proffered their sympathies to her, Colin was the only one who had no pity upon the poor child. If Marietta was talked of he became as dumb as a fish. If he met her in the street he would turn red and white with anger, and cast sidelong glances at her of the most malicious kind.

If at evening the young people met upon the seashore near the old castle ruins for sprightly pastimes, or rural dances, or to sing catches, Colin was the merriest among them. But as soon as Marietta arrived the rascally fellow was silent, and all the gold in the world couldn't make him sing.—What a pity, when he had such a fine voice! Everybody listened to it so willingly, and its store of songs was endless.

All the maidens looked kindly upon Colin, and he was friendly with all of them. He had, as we have said, a roguish glance, which the lasses feared and loved; and it was so sweet they would like to have had it painted. But, as might naturally be expected, the offended Marietta did not look graciously upon him. And in that he was perfectly right. Whether he smiled or not, it was all the same to her. As to his roguish glance, why she would never hear it mentioned; and therein too she was perfectly right. When he told a tale (and he knew thousands) and everybody listened, she nudged her neighbor, or perhaps threw tufts of grass at Peter or Paul, and laughed and chattered, and did not listen to Colin at all. This behavior quite provoked the proud fellow, so that he would break off in the middle of his story and stalk sullenly away.

Revenge is sweet. The daughter of Mother Manon well knew how to triumph. Yet Marietta was a right good child and quite too tenderhearted. If Colin was silent, it gave her pain. If he was downcast, she laughed no more. If he went away, she did not stay long behind: but hurried to her home, and wept tears of repentance, more beautiful than those of the Magdalen, although she had not sinned like the Magdalen.

THE CUP.

Father Jerome, the pastor of Napoule, was an old man of seventy, who possessed all the virtues of a saint, and only one failing; which was, that by reason of his advanced years, he was hard of hearing. But, on that very account, his homilies were more acceptable to the children of his baptism and blessing. True, he preached only of two subjects, as if they comprehended the whole of religion. It was either "Little children, love one another," or it was "Mysterious are the ways of Providence." And truly there is so much Faith, Love, and Hope in these that one might at a pinch be saved by them. The little children loved one another most obediently, and trusted in the ways of Providence. Only Colin, with his flinty heart, would know nothing of either: for even when he professed to be friendly, he entertained the deepest malice.

The Napoulese went to the annual market or fair of the city of Vence. It was truly a joyful time, and though they had but little gold to buy with, there were many goods to look at. Now Marietta and Mother Manon went to the fair with the rest, and Colin was also there. He bought a great many curiosities and trifles for his friends—but he would not spend a farthing for Marietta. And yet he was always at her elbow, though he did not speak to her, nor she to him. It was easy to see that he was brooding over some scheme of wickedness.

Mother Manon stood gazing before a shop, when she suddenly exclaimed:

"Oh! Marietta, see that beautiful cup! A queen would not be ashamed to raise it to her lips. Only see: the edge is of dazzling gold, and the flowers upon it could not bloom more beautifully in the garden, although they are only painted. And in the midst of this Paradise! pray see, Marietta, how the apples are smiling on the trees. They are verily tempting. And Adam cannot withstand it, as the enchanting Eve offers him one for food! And do see how prettily the little frisking lamb skips around the old tiger, and the snow-white dove with her golden throat stands there before the vulture, as if she would caress him."

Marietta could not satisfy herself with looking. "Had I such a cup, mother!" said she, "it is far too beautiful to drink out of: I would place my flowers in it and constantly peep into Paradise. We are at the fair in Vence, but when I look on the picture I feel as if I were in Paradise."

So spoke Marietta, and called her companions to the spot, to share her admiration of the cup: but the young men soon joined the maidens, until at length almost half the inhabitants of Napoule were assembled before the wonderfully beautiful cup. But miraculously beautiful was it mainly from its inestimable, translucent porcelain, with gilded handles and glowing colors. They asked the merchant timidly: "Sir, what is the price of it?" And he answered: "Among friends, it is worth a hundred livres." Then they all became silent, and went away in despair. When the Napoulese were all gone from the front of the shop, Colin came there by stealth, threw the merchant a hundred livres upon the counter, had the cup put in a box well packed with cotton, and then carried it off. What evil plans he had in view no one would have surmised.

Near Napoule, on his way home, it being already dusk, he met old Jacques, the Justice's servant, returning from the fields. Jacques was a very good man, but excessively stupid.

"I will give thee money enough to get something to drink, Jacques," said Colin, "if thou wilt bear this box to Manon's house, and leave it there; and if any one should see thee, and inquire from whom the box came, say 'A stranger gave it to me.' But never disclose my name, or I will always detest thee."

Jacques promised this, took the drink-money and the box, and went with it toward the little dwelling between the olive trees and the African acacias.

THE CARRIER.

Before he arrived there he encountered his master, Justice Hautmartin, who asked; "Jacques, what art thou carrying?"

"A box for Mother Manon. But, sir, I cannot say from whom it comes."

"Why not?"

"Because Colin would always detest me."

"It is well that thou canst keep a secret. But it is already late; give me the box, for I am going to-morrow to see Mother Manon; I will deliver it to her and not betray that it came from Colin. It will save thee a walk, and furnish me a good excuse for calling on the old lady."

Jacques gave the box to his master, whom he was accustomed to obey implicitly in all things. The justice bore it into his chamber, and examined it by the light with some curiosity. On the lid was neatly written with red chalk: "For the lovely and dear Marietta." But Monsieur Hautmartin well knew that this was some of Colin's mischief, and that some knavish trick lurked under the whole. He therefore opened the box carefully for fear that a mouse or rat should be concealed within. When he beheld the wondrous cup, which he had seen at Vence, he was dreadfully shocked, for Monsieur Hautmartin was a skilful casuist, and knew that the inventions and devices of the human heart are evil from our youth upward. He saw at once that Colin designed this cup as a means of bringing misfortune upon Marietta: perhaps to give out, when it should be in her possession, that it was the present of some successful lover in the town, or the like, so that all decent people would thereafter keep aloof from Marietta. Therefore Monsieur Hautmartin resolved, in order to prevent any evil reports, to profess himself the giver. Moreover, he loved Marietta, and would gladly have seen her observe more strictly toward himself the sayings of the gray-headed priest Jerome, "Little children, love one another." In truth, Monsieur Hautmartin was a little child of fifty years old, and Marietta did not think the saying applied particularly to him. Mother Manon, on the contrary, thought that the justice was a clever little child, he had gold and a high reputation from one end of Napoule to the other. And when the justice spoke of marriage, and Marietta ran away in affright, Mother Manon remained sitting, and had no fear for the tall, staid gentleman. It must also be confessed there were no faults in his person. And although Colin might be the handsomest man in the village, yet the justice far surpassed him in two things, namely, in the number of years, and in a very, very big nose. Yes, this nose, which always went before the justice like a herald to proclaim his approach, was a real elephant among human noses.

With this proboscis, his good purpose, and the cup, the justice went the following morning to the house between the olive trees and the African acacias.

"For the beautiful Marietta," said he, "I hold nothing too costly. Yesterday you admired the cup at Vence; to-day allow me, lovely Marietta, to lay it and my devoted heart at your feet."

Manon and Marietta were transported beyond measure when they beheld the cup. Manon's eyes glistened with delight, but Marietta turned and said: "I can neither take your heart nor your cup."

Then Mother Marion was angry, and cried out: "But I accept both heart and cup. Oh, thou little fool, how long wilt thou despise thy good fortune! For whom dost thou tarry? Will a count of Provence make thee his bride, that thou scornest the Justice of Napoule? I know better how to look after my interests. Monsieur Hautmartin, I deem it an honor to call thee my son-in-law."

Then Marietta went out and wept bitterly, and hated the beautiful cup with all her heart.

But the justice, drawing the palm of his flabby hand over his nose, spoke thus judiciously:

"Mother Manon, hurry nothing. The dove will at length, when it learns to know me better, give way. I am not impetuous. I have some skill among women, and before a quarter of a year passes by I will insinuate myself into Marietta's good graces."

"Thy nose is too large for that," whispered Marietta, who listened outside the door and laughed to herself. In fact, the quarter of a year passed by and Monsieur Hautmartin had not yet pierced the heart even with the tip of his nose.

THE FLOWERS.

During this quarter of a year Marietta had other affairs to attend to. The cup gave her much vexation and trouble, and something else besides.

For a fortnight nothing else was talked of in Napoule, and every one said it is a present from the justice, and the marriage is already agreed upon. Marietta solemnly declared to all her companions that she would rather plunge to the bottom of the sea than marry the justice, but the maidens continued to banter her all the more, saying: "Oh, how blissful it must be to repose in the shadow of his nose!" This was her first vexation.

Then Mother Manon had the cruelty to force Marietta to rinse out the cup every morning at the spring under the rock and to fill it with fresh flowers. She hoped by this to accustom Marietta to the cup and heart of the giver. But Marietta continued to hate both the gift and giver, and her work at the spring became an actual punishment.

Second vexation.

Then, when in the morning, she came to the spring, twice every week she found on the rock, immediately over it, some most beautiful flowers, handsomely arranged, all ready for the decoration of the cup. And on the flower-stalks a strip of paper was always tied, on which was written, "Dear Marietta." Now no one need expect to impose upon little Marietta as if magicians and fairies were still in the world. Consequently she knew that both the flowers and papers must have come from Monsieur Hautmartin. Marietta, indeed, would not smell them because the living breath from out of the justice's nose had perfumed them. Nevertheless she took the flowers, because they were finer than wild flowers, and tore the slip of paper into a thousand pieces, which she strewed upon the spot where the flowers usually lay. But this did not vex Justice Hautmartin, whose love was unparalleled in its kind as his nose was in its kind. Third vexation.

At length it came out in conversation with Monsieur Hautmartin that he was not the giver of the beautiful flowers. Then who could it be? Marietta was utterly astounded at the unexpected discovery. Thenceforth she took the flowers from the rock more kindly; but, further, Marietta was—what maidens are not wont to be—very inquisitive. She conjectured first this and then that young man in Napoule. Yet her conjectures were in vain. She looked and listened far into the night; she rose earlier than usual But she looked and listened in vain. And still twice a week in the morning the miraculous flowers lay upon the rock, and upon the strip of paper wound round them she always read the silent sigh, "Dear Marietta!" Such an incident would have made even the most indifferent inquisitive. But curiosity at length became a burning pain. Fourth vexation.

WICKEDNESS UPON WICKEDNESS.

Now Father Jerome, on Sunday, had again preached from the text: "Mysterious are the dispensations of Providence." And little Marietta thought, if Providence would only dispense that I might at length find out who is the flower dispenser. Father Jerome was never wrong.

On a summer night, when it was far too warm to rest, Marietta awoke very early, and could not resume her sleep. Therefore she sprang joyously from her couch as the first streaks of dawn flashed against the window of her little chamber, over the waves of the sea and the Lerinian Isles, dressed herself, and went out to wash her forehead, breast, and arms in the cool spring. She took her hat with her, intending to take a walk by the sea-shore, as she knew of a retired place for bathing.

In order to reach this retired spot, it was necessary to pass over the rocks behind the house, and thence down through the orange and palm trees. On this occasion Marietta could not pass through them; for, under the youngest and most slender of the palms lay a tall young man in profound sleep—near him a nosegay of most splendid flowers. A white paper lay thereon, from which probably a sigh was again breathing. How could Marietta get by there?

She stood still, trembling with fright. She would go home again. Hardly had she retreated a couple of steps, ere she looked again at the sleeper and remained motionless. Yet the distance prevented her from recognizing his face. Now the mystery was to be solved, or never. She tripped lightly nearer to the palms; but he seemed to stir—then she ran again toward the cottage. His movements were but the fearful imaginings of Marietta. Now she returned again on her way toward the palms; but his sleep might perhaps be only dissembled—swiftly she ran toward the cottage—but who would flee for a mere probability? She trod more boldly the path toward the palms.

With these fluctuations of her timid and joyous spirit, between fright and curiosity, with these to-and-fro trippings between the house and the palm-trees, she at length nearly approached the sleeper; at the same time curiosity became more powerful than fear.

"What is he to me? My way leads me directly past him. Whether he sleeps or wakes, I will go straight on." So thought Manon's daughter. But she passed not by, but stood looking directly in the face of the flower-giver, in order to be certain who it was. Besides, he slept as if it were the first time in a month. And who was it? Now, who else should it be but the archwicked Colin.

14

So it was *he* who had annoyed the gentle maiden, and given her so much trouble with Monsieur Hautmartin, because he bore a grudge against her; he had been the one who had teased her with flowers, in order to torture her curiosity. Wherefore? He hated Marietta. He behaved himself always most shamefully toward the poor child. He avoided her when he could; and when he could not, he grieved the good-natured little one. With all the other maidens of Napoule he was more chatty, friendly, courteous, than toward Marietta. Consider—he had never once asked her to dance, and yet she danced bewitchingly.

Now there he lay, surprised, taken in the act. Revenge swelled in Marietta's bosom. What disgrace could she subject him to? She took the nosegay, unloosened it, strewed his present over the sleeper in scorn. But the paper, on which appeared again the sigh, "Dear Marietta!" she retained, and thrust quickly into her bosom. She wished to preserve this proof of his handwriting. Marietta was sly. Now she would go away. But her revenge was not yet satisfied. She could not leave the place without returning Colin's ill-will.

She took the violet-colored silken ribbon from her hat, and threw it lightly around the sleeper's arm and around the tree, and with three knots tied Colin fast. Now when he awoke, how astonished he would be! How his curiosity would torment him to ascertain who had played him this trick! He could not possibly know. So much the better; it served him right. She seemed to regret her work when she had finished it. Her bosom throbbed impetuously. Indeed, I believe that a little tear filled her eye, as she compassionately gazed upon the guilty one. Slowly she retreated to the orange grove by the rocks—she looked around often—slowly ascended the rocks, looking down among the palm trees as she ascended. Then she hastened to Mother Manon, who was calling her.

THE HAT BAND.

That very day Colin practised new mischief. What did he? He wished to shame the poor Marietta publicly. Ah! she never thought that every one in Napoule knew her violet-colored ribbon! Colin remembered it but too well. Proudly he bound it around his hat, and exhibited it to the gaze of all the world as a conquest. And male and female cried out: "He has received it from Marietta."—And all the maidens said angrily: "The reprobate!" And all the young men who liked to see Marietta cried out: "The reprobate!"

"How! Mother Manon?" shrieked the Justice Hautmartin when he came to her house, and he shrieked so loudly that it re-echoed wonderfully through his nose. "How! do you suffer this? my betrothed presents the young proprietor Colin with her hat-band! It is high time that we celebrate our nuptials. When that is over, then I shall have a right to speak."

"You have a right!" answered Mother Manon, "if things are so, the marriage must take place forthwith. When that is done, all will go right."

"But, Mother Manon, Marietta always refuses to give me her consent."

"Prepare the marriage feast."

"But she will not even look kindly at me; and when I seat myself at her side, the little savage jumps up and runs away."

"Justice, only prepare the marriage feast."

"But if Marietta resists—"

"We will take her by surprise. We will go to Father Jerome on Monday morning early, and he shall quietly celebrate the marriage. This we can easily accomplish with him. I am her mother, you the first judicial person in Napoule. He must obey. Marietta need know nothing about it. Early on Monday morning I will send her to Father Jerome all alone, with a message so that she will suspect nothing. Then the priest shall speak earnestly to her. Half an hour afterward we two will come. Then swiftly to the altar. And even if Marietta should then say No, what does it matter? The old Priest can hear nothing. But till then, mum to Marietta and all Napoule."

So the secret remained with the two. Marietta dreamed not of the good luck which was in store for her. She thought only of Colin's wickedness, which had made her the common talk of the whole place. Oh! how she repented her heedlessness about the ribbon; and yet in her heart she forgave the reprobate his crime. Marietta was far too good. She told her mother, she told all her playmates, "Colin has found my lost hat band. I never gave it to him. He only wishes to vex me with it. You all know that Colin was always ill-disposed towards me, and always sought to mortify me!"

Ah! the poor child! she knew not what new abomination the malicious fellow was again contriving.

THE BROKEN CUP.

Early in the morning Marietta went to the spring with the cup. There were no flowers yet on the rock. It was still quite too early; for the sun had scarcely risen from the sea.

Footsteps were heard. Colin came in sight, the flowers in his hand. Marietta became very red. Colin stammered out "good morning, Marietta," but the greeting came not from his heart, he could hardly bring it over his lips.

"Why dost thou wear my ribbon so publicly, Colin?" said Marietta, and placed the cup upon the rock. "I did not give it thee."

"Thou didst not give it to me, dear Marietta?" asked he, and inward rage made him deadly pale.

Marietta was ashamed of the falsehood, drooped her eyelids, and said after a while, "Well, I did give it to thee, yet thou shouldst not have worn it so openly. Give it me back again."

Slowly he untied it; his anger was so great that he could not prevent the tears from filling his eyes, nor the sighs from escaping his breast.—"Dear Marietta, leave thy ribbon with me," said he softly.

"No," answered she.

Then his suppressed passion changed into desperation. Sighing, he looked towards Heaven, then sadly on Marietta, who, silent and abashed, stood by the spring with downcast eyes.

He wound the violet coloured ribbon around the stalks of the flowers, said "there, take them all," and threw the flowers so spitefully against the magnificent cup upon the rock, that it was thrown down and dashed to pieces. Maliciously he fled away.

Mother Manon lurking behind the window, had seen and heard all. When the cup broke, hearing and sight left her. She was scarcely able to speak for very horror. And as she pushed with all her strength against the narrow window, to shout after the guilty one, it gave way, and with one crash fell to the earth and was shattered in pieces.

So much ill luck would have discomposed any other woman. But Manon soon recovered herself. "How lucky that I was a witness to this roguery!" exclaimed she; "he must to the Justice.—He shall replace both cup and window-sash with his gold. It will give a rich dowry to Marietta But when Marietta brought in the fragments of the shattered cup, when Manon saw the

Paradise lost, the good man Adam without a head, and of Eve not a solitary limb remaining, the serpent unhurt, triumphing, the tiger safe, but the little lamb gone even to the very tail, as if the tiger had swallowed it, then Mother Manon screamed forth curses against Colin, and said: 'One can easily see that this *fall* came from the hand of the devil.'"

THE TRIBUNAL.

She took the cup in one hand, Marietta in the other, and went, about nine o'clock, to when Monsieur Hautmartin was wont to sit in judgment. She there made a great outcry, and showed the broken cup and the Paradise lost. Marietta wept bitterly.

The justice, when he saw the broken cup and his beautiful bride in tears, flew into so violent a rage toward Colin that his nose was as violet-colored as Marietta's well-known hat-band, He immediately despatched his bailiffs to bring the criminal before him.

Colin came, overwhelmed with grief. Mother Manon now repeated her complaint with great eloquence before justice, bailiffs, and scribes.—But Colin listened not. He stepped to Marietta and whispered to hen "Forgive me, dear Marietta, as I forgive thee. I broke thy cup unintentionally; but thou, thou hast broken my heart!"

"What whispering is that?" cried Justice Hautmartin, with magisterial authority. "Harken to this accusation, and defend yourself."

"I have naught to defend. I broke the cup against my will," said Colin.

"That I verily believe," said Marietta, sobbing. "I am as guilty as he; for I offended him—then he threw the ribbon and flowers to me. He could not help it."

"Well!" cried Mother Manon. "Do you intend to defend him? Mr. Justice, pronounce his sentence. He has broken the cup, and he does not deny it."

"Since you cannot deny it, Mr. Colin," said the Justice, "you must pay three hundred livres for the cup, for it is worth that; and then for—"

"No," interrupted Colin, "it is not worth that. I bought it at Vence for Marietta for a hundred livres."

"You bought it, sir brazen face?" shrieked the Justice, and his whole face became like Marietta's hat-hand. He could not and would not say more, for he dreaded a disagreeable investigation of the matter.

But Colin was vexed at the imputation, and said: "I sent this cup on the evening of the fair, by your own servant, to Marietta. There stands Jacques in the door. Speak, Jacques, did I not give thee the box to carry to Mother Manon?"

Monsieur Hautmartin wished to interrupt this conversation by speaking loudly. But the simple Jacques said: "Only recollect, Justice, you took away Colin's box from me, and carried what was in it to Mother Manon. The box lies there under the papers."

Then the bailiffs were ordered to remove the simpleton; and Colin was also directed to retire, until he should be sent for again.

"Very well, Mr. Justice," interposed Colin, "but this business shall be your last in Napoule. I know this, that you would ingratiate yourself with Mother Manon and Marietta by means of my property. When you want me, you will have to ride to Grasse to the Governor's." With that, Colin departed.

Monsieur Hautmartin was quite puzzled with this affair, and in his confusion knew not what he was about. Manon shook her head. The affair was dark and mysterious to her. "Who will now pay me for the broken cup?" she asked.

"To me," said Marietta, with glowing, brightened countenance, "*to me* it is already paid for."

MYSTERIOUS DISPENSATIONS.

Colin rode that same day to the Governor at Grasse, and came back early the next morning. But Justice Hautmartin only laughed at him, and removed all of Mother Manon's suspicions by swearing he would let his nose be cut off if Colin did not pay three hundred livres for the broken cup. He also went with Mother Manon to talk with Father Jerome about the marriage, and impressed upon him the necessity of earnestly setting before Marietta her duty *as* an obedient daughter in not opposing the will of her mother. This the pious old man promised, although he understood not the half of what they shouted in his ear.

When Monday morning came Mother Manon said to her daughter: "Dress yourself handsomely, and carry this myrtle wreath to Father Jerome; he wants it for a bride." Marietta dressed herself in her Sunday clothes, took the myrtle wreath unsuspiciously, and carried it to Father Jerome.

On the way Colin met her, and greeted her joyfully, though timidly; and when she told him where she was taking the wreath, Colin said: "I am going the same way, for I am carrying the money for the church's tenths to the priest." And as they went on he took her hand silently, and both trembled as if they designed some crime against each other.

"Hast thou forgiven me?" whispered Colin, anxiously. "Ah! Marietta, what have I done to thee, that thou art so cruel toward me?"

She could only say: "Be quiet, Colin, you shall have the ribbon again; and I will preserve the cup since it came from you! Did it really come from you?"

"Ah! Marietta, canst thou doubt it? All I have I would gladly give thee. Wilt thou, hereafter, be as kind to me as thou art to others?"

She replied not. But as she entered the parsonage she looked aside at him, and when she saw his fine eyes filled with tears, she whispered softly: "Dear Colin!" Then he bent down and kissed her hand. With this the door of a chamber opened and Father Jerome, with venerable aspect, stood before them. The young couple held fast to each other. I know not whether this was the effect of the hand-kissing, or the awe they felt for the sage.

Marietta handed him the myrtle wreath. He laid it upon her head and said: "Little children, love one another;" and then urged the good maiden, in the most touching and pathetic manner, to love Colin. For the old gentleman, from his hardness of hearing, had either mistaken the name of the bridegroom, or forgotten it, and thought Colin must be the bridegroom.

Then Marietta's heart softened under the exhortation, and with tears and sobs she exclaimed: "Ah! I have loved him for a long time, but he hates me."

"I hate thee, Marietta?" cried Colin. "My soul has lived only in thee since thou earnest to Napoule. Oh! Marietta, how could I hope and believe that thou didst love me? Does not all Napoule worship thee?"

"Why, then, dost thou avoid me, Colin, and prefer all my companions before me?"

"Oh! Marietta, I feared and trembled with love and anxiety when I beheld thee; I had not the courage to approach thee; and when I was away from thee I was most miserable."

As they talked thus with each other the good father thought they were quarreling; and he threw his arms around them, brought them together, and said imploringly: "Little children, love one another."

Then Marietta sank on Colin's breast, and Colin threw his arms around her, and both faces beamed with rapture. They forgot the priest, the whole world. Each was sunk into the other, Both had so completely lost their recollection that, unwittingly, they followed the delightful Father Jerome into the church and before the altar.

"Marietta!" sighed he.

"Colin!" sighed she.

In the church there were many devout worshipers; but they witnessed Colin's and Marietta's marriage with amazement. Many ran out before the close of the ceremony, to spread the news throughout Napoule: "Colin and Marietta are married."

When the solemnization was over, Father Jerome rejoiced that he had succeeded so well, and that such little opposition had been made by the parties. He led them into the parsonage.

END OF THIS MEMORABLE HISTORY.

Then Mother Manon arrived, breathless; she had waited at home a long time for the bride-groom. He had not arrived. At the last stroke of the clock she grew anxious and went to Monsieur Hautmartin's. There anew surprise awaited her. She learned that the Governor, together with the officers of the Viguerie, had appeared and taken possession of the accounts, chests, and papers of the justice and at the same time arrested Monsieur Hautmartin.

"This, surely, is the work of that wicked Colin," thought she, and hurried to the parsonage in order to apologize to Father Jerome for delaying the marriage. The good gray-headed old man advanced toward her, proud of his work, and leading by the hand the newly married pair.

Now Mother Manon lost her wits and her speech in good earnest when she learned what had happened. But Colin had more thoughts and power of speech than in his whole previous life. He told of his love and the broken cup, the falsehood of the justice, and how he had unmasked this unjust magistrate in the Viguerie at Grasse. Then he besought Mother Manon's blessing, since all this had happened without any fault on the part of Marietta or himself.

Father Jerome, who for a long while could not make out what had happened, when he received a full explanation of the marriage through mistake, piously folded his hands and exclaimed, with uplifted eyes: "Wonderful are the dispensations of Providence!" Colin and Marietta kissed his hands; Mother Manon, through sheer veneration of heaven, gave the young couple her blessing, but remarked incidentally that her head seemed turned round.

Mother Manon herself was pleased with her son-in-law when she came to know the full extent of his property, and especially when she found that Monsieur Hautmartin and his nose had been arrested.

"But am I then really a wife?" asked Marietta; "and really Colin's wife?"

Mother Manon nodded her head, and Marietta hung upon Colin's arm. Thus they went to Colin's farm, to his dwelling-house, through the garden.

"Look at the flowers, Marietta," said Colin; "how carefully I cultivated them for your cup!"

Colin, who had not expected so pleasant an event, now prepared a wedding feast on the spur of the occasion. Two days was it continued. All Napoule was feasted. Who shall describe Colin's extravagance?

The broken cup is preserved in the family to the present day as a memorial and sacred relic.